This Orchard book

belongs to

....

TEN LITTLE MONKEYS

MIKE BROWNLOW   SIMON RICKERTY

ORCHARD

Ten little monkeys, sitting in a tree,
Feeling full of mischief, giggling with glee.

Time to have some jungle fun! What d'you think they'll do?
Ten little monkeys say,

"HOO-HAA-HOO!"

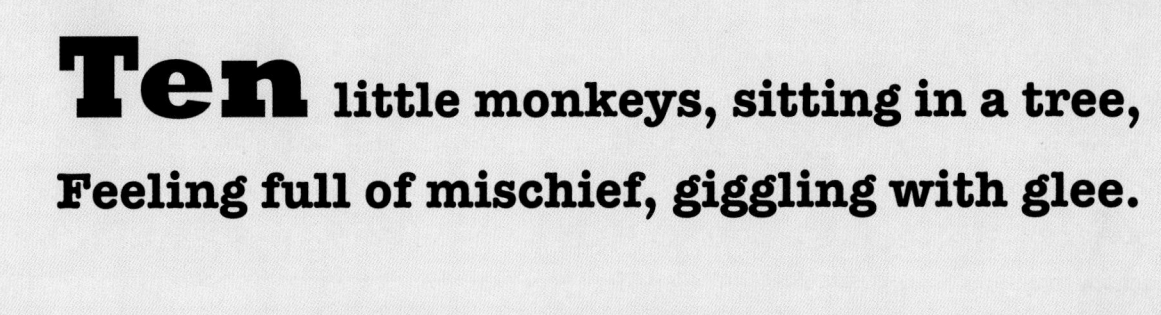

10 **Ten** little monkeys swing from vine to vine.

WHEEEE! Giraffes to slide down! Now there are . . .

. . . nine.

9

Nine little monkeys
leave hippo in a state.

SPLAT!

goes the squelchy mud.

Now there are . . .

...eight.

Eight little monkeys
dance in disco heaven!

BOOM!

8

BOOM!

go the jungle drums.

Now there are . . .

...seven.

Seven little monkeys,
playing cheeky tricks.

7

THRRPPPPP!

go the meerkats.

Now there are . . .

Six little monkeys swim
and splash and dive.

6

SPLOOSH!

go the elephants.

Now there are . . .

...five.

Five little monkeys play a tug of war.

5

HISSS! goes the angry snake.

Now there are . . .

. . . four.

Four little monkeys

leap from tree to tree.

4

SNAP!

goes the crocodile!

Now there are . . .

...three.

Three little monkeys cause a right to-do!

3

ROAR!

growls the lion pack.

Now there are . . .

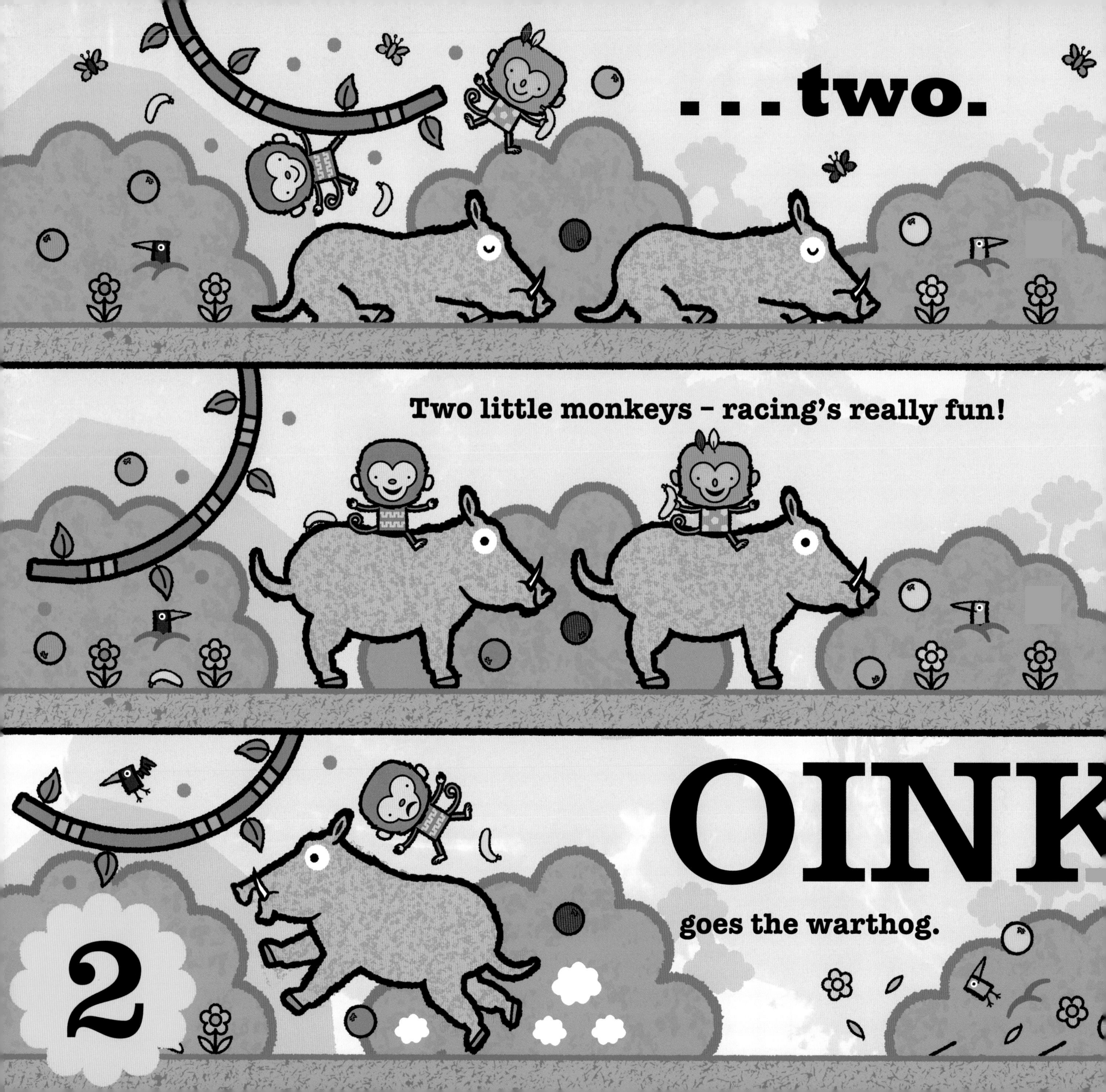

. . . **two.**

Two little monkeys – racing's really fun!

OINK

goes the warthog.

2

KKK!

Now there's only . . .

One little monkey,
sitting on a stone.

How can he have fun and games,
now he's all alone?

But look who's here
– it's Granny Ape!
She's found them
all somehow.

"You cheeky monkeys," Granny says,

"It's time for bed right now!"

Ten little monkeys - a tired little crew.

Tucked up tight with happy dreams.

"HOO-HAA-HOO!"

For Toby, Emily and Rex – our own little monkeys!
M.B.

For Erin and Isla
S.R.

ORCHARD BOOKS

First published in Great Britain in 2020 by The Watts Publishing Group

1 3 5 7 9 10 8 6 4 2

Text © Mike Brownlow, 2020
Illustrations © Simon Rickerty, 2020

A CIP catalogue record for this book is available from the British Library.

ISBN 978 1 40835 589 3

Printed and bound in Italy

Orchard Books
An imprint of Hachette Children's Group
Part of The Watts Publishing Group Limited
Carmelite House
50 Victoria Embankment
London EC4Y 0DZ

An Hachette UK Company
www.hachette.co.uk

www.hachettechildrens.co.uk